Time for Lunch

by Ron Heath
illustrated by Paul Meisel

"It's time for lunch,"
said Mother Bear.
"Baby Bear likes berries.
I will get some berries."

3

Mother Bear
got some berries.
"Yum, yum,"
said Mother Bear.
"I like berries, too."

"Little Bear likes nuts,"
said Mother Bear.
"I will get some nuts."

Mother Bear
got some nuts.
"Yum, yum,"
said Mother Bear.
"I like nuts, too."

9

"Father Bear likes fish,"
said Mother Bear.
"I will get some fish."

Mother Bear got some fish.
"I like fish, too,"
said Mother Bear.

"I like honey,"
said Mother Bear.
"I will get some honey."

Mother Bear
got some honey.

"Oh, no!" said Mother Bear.

Mother Bear ran.
She ran and ran.

"Yum, yum,"
said Mother Bear.
"I like honey.
But I do **not**
like bees!"

16